MY FIRST BOOK ABOUT SWEDEN

Min första bok om Sverige

LINDA LIEBRAND

Sverige
Sweden

Faluröd stuga
Falu red cottage

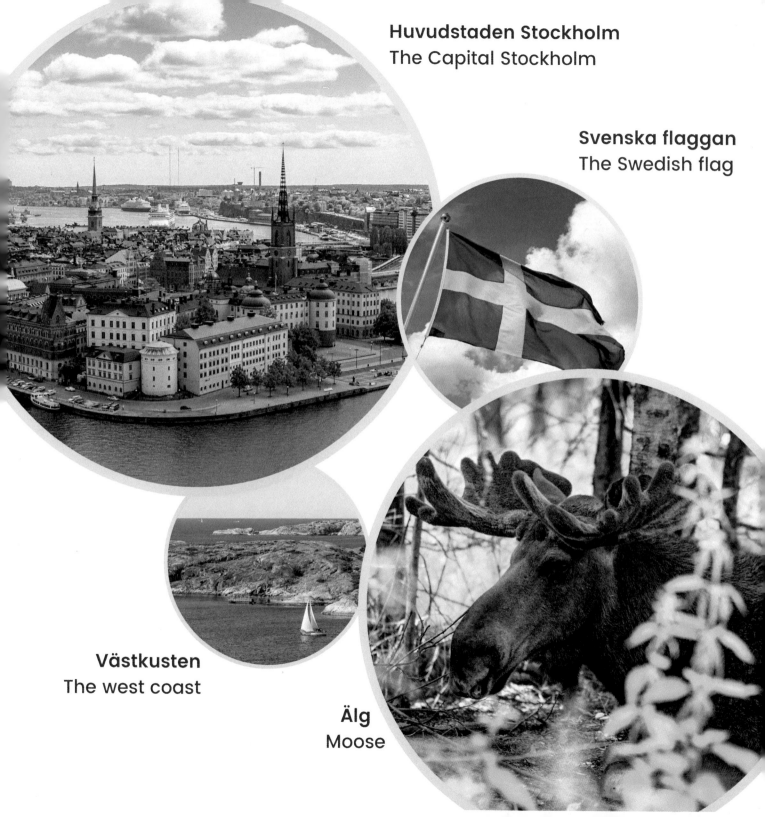

Huvudstaden Stockholm
The Capital Stockholm

Svenska flaggan
The Swedish flag

Västkusten
The west coast

Älg
Moose

Midsommarfest
Midsummer party

Midsommarstång
Midsummer pole

Prästkragar
Daisies

Jordgubbstårta
Strawberry cake

Midsommarkrans
Midsummer wreath

Nära Naturen
Close to Nature

Roddbåt
Rowing boat

Plocka blommor
Picking flowers

Stranden
The beach

Klättra i träd
Climbing trees

Tälta
Camping

I naturens skafferi
In nature's pantry

Korg
Basket

Smultron
Wild strawberries

Kantareller
Chanterelles

Blåbär
Blueberries

Fisk (Abborre)
Fish (Perch)

Välkommen Vinter
Welcome Winter

Snögubbe
Snowman

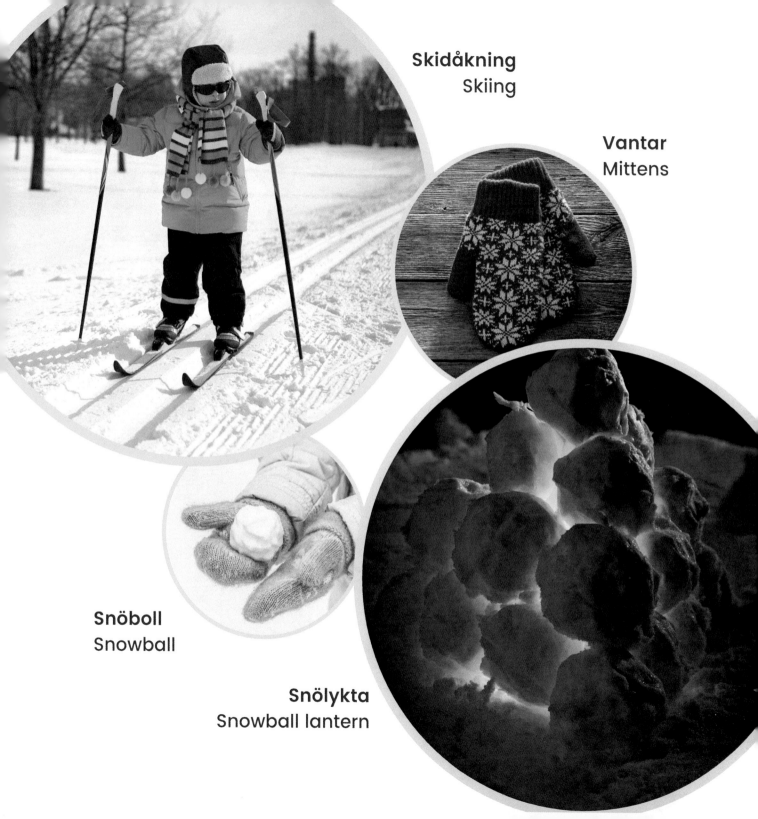

Skidåkning
Skiing

Vantar
Mittens

Snöboll
Snowball

Snölykta
Snowball lantern

Vi firar lucia
We're celebrating lucia

Adventsljusstaken
Advent candlestick

Pepparkaksgubbar
Gingerbread men

Lussekatter
Saffron buns

Lucia
Lucia

Luciatåg
Lucia parade

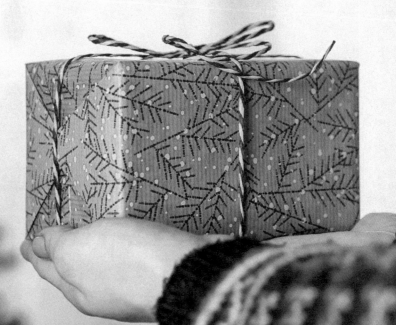

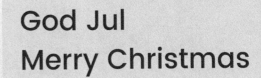

God Jul
Merry Christmas

Julklapp
Christmas present

Tomte och julgran
Santa and Christmas tree

Julmat
Christmas food

Adventsljusstake
Advent candlestick

Julbock
Yule goat

Äntligen vår!
Finally spring!

Snödroppar
Snowdrops

Påskkärring - Easter witch
Glad Påsk - Happy Easter

Påskägg
Easter egg

Påskris
Easter twigs

Vitsippor
Anemones

Typiskt svenskt
Typically Swedish

Älgskylt
Moose sign

Dalahäst
Dala horse

Lördagsgodis
Saturday sweets

Student mössa
Graduation cap

Renar
Reindeer

Vikingatiden
The Viking period

Runsten
Rune stone

Vikingaskepp
Viking ship

Vikingahjälm
Viking helmet

Vikingasköld
Viking shield

Det är fika dags
It's fika time

Kopp
Cup

Kanelbullar
Cinnamon rolls

Prinsesstårta
Princess cake

Dammsugare
Punch rolls

Semla
Shrovetide bun

Smaklig Måltid
Bon appetit

Köttbullar med potatismos och lingonsylt
Meatballs with mash and lingonberry jam

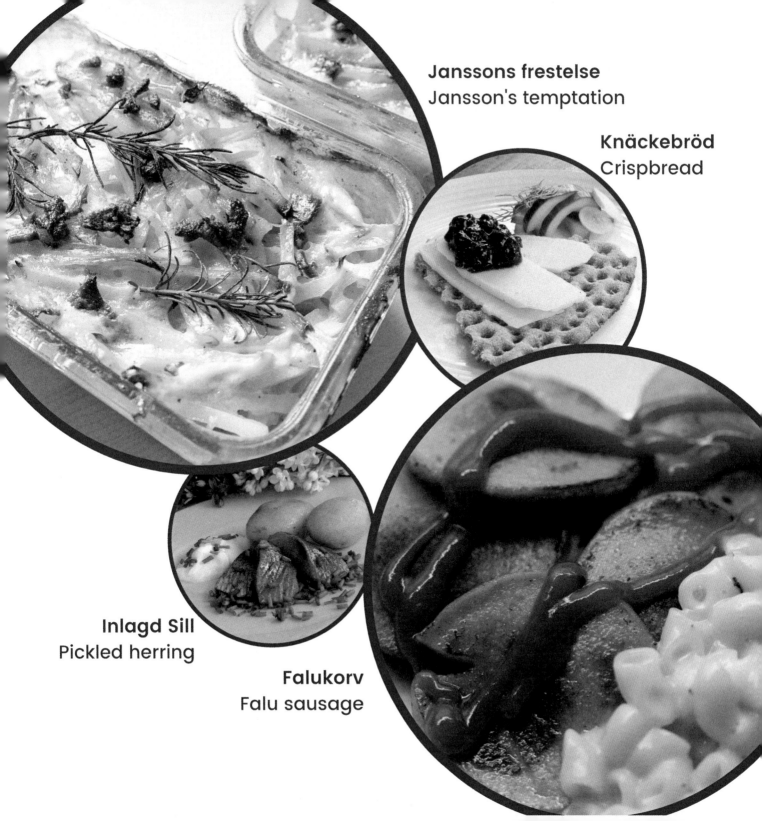

Janssons frestelse
Jansson's temptation

Knäckebröd
Crispbread

Inlagd Sill
Pickled herring

Falukorv
Falu sausage

mamma
mum

bebis
baby

Hej, Hello!

Hi. I'm Linda. I'm a Swedish mum living among the rolling green hills of Surrey in the United Kingdom, together with my Dutch husband, bouncy toddler and boisterous Swiss dog.

I write bilingual children's books to share my native language and some Swedish culture with my little boy.

I'd love to stay in touch! Sign up for my newsletter at www.Swenglish.life and I'll email you a free bilingual e-book. And while you're on my website - be sure to check out the latest Swedish language resources for bilingual kids.

I've created writing exercises, colouring books, story books and so much more to help you teach your kids Swedish abroad.

Want more Bilingual Books?

Count all things Swedish!

8
Åtta flaggor
Eight flags

Den svenska flaggan är blå och gul. Vi firar svenska flaggans dag och Sveriges nationaldag den 6 juni.

The Swedish flag is blue and yellow. We celebrate the Swedish flag and our National Day on 6 June.

Counting Sweden
RÄKNA MED SVERIGE

Linda Liebrand

'Counting Sweden – Räkna med Sverige'
One Midsummer pole, two Vikings or three crowns? Just imagine how many typically Swedish things there are to count!
www.swenglish.life

Colour and Learn Swedish!

Your kids will have hours of fun colouring and learning new Swedish words with these bilingual colouring books.
Available in traditional paperback format from book stores, and printable PDF download from www.swenglish.life

Lupiner
Lupines

First Printing, 2018
Treetop Media Ltd

Book cover: Midsummer girl By © Juta via Shutterstock, Wild strawberries By © Monika Gniot via Shutterstock, Cinnamon rolls By © Susanna Svensson via Shutterstock, Dala horse By © KhunYing via Shutterstock. Pg 1: Wild strawberries by By © HHelene via Shutterstock. Pg 2: Falu red cottage by © By ale_rizzo via Shutterstock. Pg 3: Stockholm By © Andrey Shcherbukhin via Shutterstock, Swedish flag By © Michael715 via Shutterstock, Westcoast by By © TTphoto via Shutterstock, Moose By © Imfoto via Shutterstock. Pg 4: Midsummer girl By © Juta via Shutterstock. Pg 5: Midsummer wreath By © bildfokus.se via Shutterstock, Daisies by © Niklas Veenhuis via Unsplash, midsummer pole By © Hans Christiansson via Shutterstock, Cake By © Kennerth Kullman via Shutterstock. Pg 6: Rowboat By © anse via Shutterstock. Pg 7: Kids picking flowers By © picturepartners via Shutterstock, Tent By © Kokhanchikov via Shutterstock, climbing tree By Petr Bonek, beach By © almgren via Shutterstock. Pg 8: Foraging By © Piotr Wawrzyniuk via Shutterstock. Pg 9: Mushrooms by By © nakhimova i via Shutterstock, girl and wild strawberries By Monika Gniot via Shutterstock, boy fishing By Piotr Wawrzyniuk via Shutterstock, blueberries By Dar1930 via Shutterstock. Pg 10: Snowman By © MNStudio via Shutterstock. Pg 11: Boy skiing © By Levranii via Shutterstock, Snowball by © Irina Sokolovskaya via Shutterstock, Snowlight By © multiart via Shutterstock, Mittens By © Maya Kruchankova via Shutterstock. Pg 12: Lucia fika By © Rikard Stadler via Shutterstock. Pg 13: Gingerbreadmen By © Kenneth Dedeu via Shutterstock, saffron buns By © bonchan via Shutterstock, Luciatåg By © bzzup via Shutterstock, Lucia girl by By © Elena. Degano via Shutterstock. Pg 14: Christmas by © JESHOOTS.COM via Unsplash. Pg 15: Santa By © Olena Hromova via Shutterstock, Jule goat By © Tommy Alven via Shutterstock, Candles By © Rikard Stadler via Shutterstock. Pg 16: Snowdrop kids By © Fotokostic via Shutterstock. Pg 17: Anemone girl By © FamVeld via Shutterstock, Easterwitch By © Anna-Mari West via Shutterstock, Easter egg By © R_Green via Shutterstock, Easter twigs By © Roland Magnusson via Shutterstock. Pg 18: Moose sign By © ABB Photo via Shutterstock. Pg 19: Sweets By © dubassy via Shutterstock, Dala horse By © KhunYing via Shutterstock, Reindeer By © nenets via Shutterstock, graduation hat By © Mikael Damkier via Shutterstock. Pg 20: Runestone By © Thomas Males via Shutterstock. Pg 21: Viking helmet girl By © Denis Val via Shutterstock, Viking shield boy By © Maria Madrinan via Shutterstock, Viking ship By © Michael Rosskothen via Shutterstock. Pg 22: Fika by © CatchaSnap via Shutterstock. Pg 23: Cinnamon rolls By © Susanna Svensson via Shutterstock, Princess cake By © Hans Geel via Shutterstock, Punch sweet rolls By © Anna Stasevska via Shutterstock, Semla by By © Vlasovalana via Shutterstock. Pg 24: Meatballs by © By Mariyana M via Shutterstock. Pg 25: Falukorv By © Emmoth via Shutterstock, Janson's temptation By © maroke via Shutterstock, Knäckebröd By © CatchaSnap via Shutterstock, Sill by © Rikard Stadler via Shutterstock. Back cover: Knäckebröd By © CatchaSnap via Shutterstock, Swedish flag By © Michael715 via Shutterstock, Falu red By © allanw via Shutterstock. This book has been designed using Canva.com.

Made in the USA
Columbia, SC
14 November 2021